my Secret Unicorn

Flying High

'I wonder what Jessica's doing now,'
she said. 'I wish I knew.'
'Me too,' Twilight said. As he spoke, his
horn touched one of the pink rocks. There
was a bright purple flash. Twilight shot
backwards with a startled whinny as mist
suddenly started to swirl over the rock.
Lauren leapt to her feet.
'Twilight!' she gasped.

My Secret Unicorn

Flying High

Linda Chapman

Illustrated by Biz Hull

PUFFIN

PUFFIN BOOKS

UK | USA | Canada | Ireland | Australia
India | New Zealand | South Africa

Puffin Books is part of the Penguin Random House group of companies
whose addresses can be found at global.penguinrandomhouse.com.

www.penguin.co.uk   www.puffin.co.uk   www.ladybird.co.uk

Penguin
Random House
UK

First published 2002
This edition published 2018

001

Written by Linda Chapman
Text copyright © Working Partners Ltd, 2002
Illustrations copyright © Biz Hull, 2002
Created by Working Partners Ltd, London W6 0QT

The moral right of the author and illustrator has been asserted

Typeset in 14.25/21.5 pt Bembo
Printed in Great Britain by Clays Ltd, St Ives plc

A CIP catalogue record for this book is available from the British Library

ISBN: 978-0-241-35425-4

All correspondence to:
Puffin Books
Penguin Random House Children's
80 Strand, London WC2R 0RL

*To Suzy Higgins – you would
be a wonderful unicorn friend*   ★
                              ★   ★

CHAPTER

One

Lauren Foster sat at the desk in her
bedroom and sighed. The sun was
just disappearing behind the Blue Ridge
Mountains and the pale sky was streaked
with pink and gold. In the paddock
behind the house, her pony, Twilight,
lifted his head and looked up. How she
wished she could be with him, but she
had work to do. When Mr Noland, her

teacher, had told the class that they were
going to do a project on the local
mountain range it had sounded like fun.
Particularly when he had said that they
could work with their friends. However,
now that she was faced with drawing a
map of all the mountains, streams and
valleys, Lauren was rapidly going off the
whole project.

She pushed her long, fair hair back
behind her ears and wondered how her
friends Mel and Jessica were getting on.
Jessica was supposed to be drawing
pictures of all the animals that lived in
the mountains and Mel was going to
write about the trees and plants that grew
there. Lauren chewed her pencil and

looked at the blank piece of paper in front of her. She had definitely got the worst deal!

It wasn't even as if she could ask her mum and dad for help. Her mum was working in the study and her dad was out at a meeting on farming. She'd checked the bookshelves but there didn't seem to be any books that might help. And she couldn't use the computer because her mum was working on it.

Lauren made up her mind. It was way too nice an evening to be inside. She could finish the map later. Jumping to her feet, she grabbed her jacket and hurried out of the room.

As she passed the bedroom of her younger brother, Max, she could hear a story-tape playing. She walked on down the corridor and put her head around the study door. 'I'm just going out to see Twilight, Mum,' she said.

Alice Foster was typing quickly, her eyes fixed on the computer screen. She was a children's author and at the moment she was in the middle of writing a new story. 'OK, honey,' she answered vaguely, not even looking round.

'Don't stay out too late.'

'I won't,' Lauren replied. With a feeling of relief, she ran down the stairs and out of the back door.

When Twilight saw Lauren coming down the path, he whinnied and trotted over to meet her.

Lauren's face broke into a smile as it always did at the sight of him. 'Hi, boy,' she said.

Twilight stamped one hoof. With his shaggy mane and scruffy dappled coat, he looked just like any other small grey pony. But he wasn't. Lauren's fingers closed around the hair from his mane that she always kept in her pocket and a familiar sense of excitement tingled through her veins. She glanced around. There was no one nearby. It was safe.

Clutching the hair, Lauren began to whisper the words she knew so well.

Twilight Star, Twilight Star,
Twinkling high above so far.
Shining light, shining bright,
Will you grant my wish tonight?
Let my little horse forlorn
Be at last a unicorn!

As Lauren spoke the final word, there

was a bright purple flash that made her shut her eyes. When she opened them again, Twilight was standing in front of her. But he wasn't a grey pony any more – he was a snowy-white unicorn.

'It worked!' Lauren exclaimed in delight. She'd said the spell many times in the past few weeks since she'd discovered Twilight's hidden powers. Even so, she still couldn't help thinking that one day nothing was going to happen.

'What were you expecting?' Twilight said with a toss of his head. His pearly-white horn caught the last rays of the setting sun and his silver mane and tail shone. He blew on her hands. 'I thought you weren't coming to see me this evening. You said you had homework to do.' His lips didn't move but Lauren could hear him clearly in her head.

'I still have got homework to do,' Lauren said. 'I've got to draw this map of the mountains. But it's really hard.' She sighed. 'I don't know what I'm going to do. I told Mel and Jessica that I'd have it done for tomorrow.'

'But that's easy,' Twilight exclaimed. 'I can fly you over the mountains and you can draw them as we go.'

Lauren stared at him. 'Really?'

'Of course,' Twilight said, tossing his mane.

Lauren grinned. 'Oh, Twilight, you're the best. Come on. Let's go!'

★

Five minutes later, Lauren and Twilight
were cantering through the sky. The wind
whipped Lauren's long hair back from
her face, but she didn't feel cold.
Twilight's silver mane swirled around her
and his body was warm. As they swooped
over the mountains, she laughed out
loud. Flying with Twilight was the
greatest feeling ever!

Lauren took a pen and paper out of
her pocket and began to draw everything
she could see. The wind pulled at the
paper and she had to hang on tight to
stop it blowing away. She was grateful for
Twilight's special unicorn magic that
stopped her from falling off.

'OK, I've drawn the river and the

valleys,' she said, straining her eyes through the gathering darkness. 'Can we go a bit lower so that I can see the trees?'

'I can do better than that,' Twilight said. 'Why don't I go low enough for you to collect some leaves from them?'

'Wow!' Lauren said in delight. 'I could stick them on to the poster next to Mel's drawings.'

Twilight cantered down through the sky and landed on the soft forest floor. Lauren picked a leaf from every different type of tree and bush she could find – pine, poplar, wild cherry, dogwood – as well as others for which she didn't know the names.

'This is great!' she said, getting back on

Twilight's back. 'Our project's going to be the best.'

As Twilight trotted forward, Lauren caught sight of two white-tailed deer, standing in the shadows of the trees. They were staring at Twilight in astonishment. Lauren grinned at the surprise on their faces.

'Where to now?' Twilight asked as he kicked with his back legs and plunged upwards. It was getting very dark.

'We'd better go home,' Lauren said reluctantly. That was the problem about riding Twilight when he was a unicorn – it was only really safe at night when they wouldn't be seen by anyone, and that meant that their rides couldn't go on for

too long. Mrs Fontana, the old lady who
had first told Lauren that unicorns
existed, had warned her that she must
never let Twilight's secret be discovered
by anyone in case it put him in danger.

'Here we go,' Twilight said, jumping
over a treetop as he cantered upwards.
'Hang on!'

Back at Granger's Farm, Twilight landed
safely in his paddock.

'Thank you!' Lauren told him, giving
him a hug.

'You're welcome,' Twilight said,
nuzzling her. 'It was fun.'

Lauren said the words of the Undoing
Spell. There was a purple flash and

suddenly Twilight was a pony again.

'Goodnight, boy,' Lauren whispered, patting him on the neck. And then she ran into the house.

To her relief, her dad wasn't back and her mum was still working. Lauren crept up the stairs and hurriedly got changed into her pyjamas. She glanced at her bedroom clock. It was nine o'clock but she didn't feel tired. That was one of the things she'd found out about flying with Twilight – she never felt tired when she got back. *Maybe it's one of his magical powers*, she thought, as she pulled the roughly drawn map out of her pocket and began to copy it on to a larger piece of paper.

As she worked, she thought about Twilight's magical powers. Mrs Fontana had told her that it was up to every unicorn to discover them for himself. Lauren and Twilight had already found out that he was able to make others feel brave when he touched them with his horn. But it was exciting to think that he might have other powers that they still hadn't discovered.

I wonder what they are, Lauren thought, as she finished drawing the last few mountains on the map. Then she heard her mum's study door open. She threw down her pencil, turned off her light and jumped into bed.

CHAPTER

Two

'This is totally brilliant!' Mel exclaimed as she looked at Lauren's map the next morning.

Lauren grinned happily. She'd got up early to finish the map off and, although it wasn't completely coloured in yet, she had to admit that it looked good. As well as the streams and valleys, she'd drawn all the different sorts of trees and plants she'd seen. 'I've got these as well,' she said, taking the leaves out of her school bag. 'I thought we could stick them on to the edges.'

'Wow!' Mel said, her brown eyes widening. 'Where did you get those from?'

'Oh . . . just around,' Lauren said vaguely. She changed the subject quickly. 'What do you think, Jessica?' she asked, looking at their other friend.

Jessica's head was lowered. She was biting her fingernails and didn't seem to hear Lauren's question.

Mel waved the map under her nose. 'Hey, Jessica. What do you think of Lauren's map?'

'Yeah, yeah – it's great,' Jessica said, not

really looking at it.

Lauren frowned. 'Are you OK?' she asked.

'I'm fine!' Jessica snapped.

Lauren and Mel exchanged surprised glances. It wasn't like Jessica to be cross.

Lauren sat down beside her. 'Want to tell us about it?' she asked in concern.

Jessica's shoulders sagged. 'I'm sorry. It's just . . . well, things aren't very good at home right now.'

'What's wrong?' Mel asked, sitting down on the other side of her.

'Sally's coming to stay for the weekend,' Jessica replied.

'But I thought you liked Sally,' Lauren said.

Jessica's mum
had died when she was little
and Sally was her dad's fiancée. They were
getting married in two weeks' time.

Jessica sighed. 'I do like her. But she's
also bringing Samantha, her daughter.
Samantha normally stays with her dad
when Sally comes to stay, but she'll be
living with us after the wedding. So Sally

thought she should come and stay this
weekend.' Jessica swallowed. 'I'm dreading
it. I know Samantha doesn't like me.'

Lauren took Jessica's hand and
squeezed it. 'I'm sure she does, Jessica. It
won't be that bad.'

Jessica looked down at the desk again.
She didn't seem convinced.

Nothing seemed to cheer Jessica up that
afternoon, not even Mr Noland telling
them that their poster was great.

At the end of the day, Lauren, Mel and
Jessica walked to the school gates
together.

'Mum, Dad and I are flying to Florida
tonight,' Mel said. 'We always go to see

my auntie and uncle every Memorial
Day weekend.'

'What about Shadow?' Lauren asked,
thinking about Mel's pony. 'Who's
looking after him?'

'Brad,' said Mel. Brad was one of the
hands who worked on her parents' farm.
'I'll miss Shadow loads, but it'll be fun
being away. Mum said we might even go
to Disneyworld! So I'll see you when I'm
back,' Mel finished, waving as she walked
over to join her parents at the gates.

'Wow!' Lauren said. She turned to see
Jessica's reaction, but Jessica hadn't heard.
She was staring straight ahead. Lauren
followed her gaze. Jessica's dad was
standing with Sally by the school gates

and with them was a slim girl who looked about eleven. She had sleek, dark-brown hair and a sulky expression on her face.

For a moment, Lauren almost thought that Jessica was going to turn round and run back into the classroom. But just then Mr Parker stepped forward.

'Jessica!' he called. 'Over here!'

Jessica had no choice but to go over. Lauren followed her.

'Hi, girls,' Sally said to them. 'Have you had a good day?'

'Yes, thanks,' Lauren said.

Jessica just nodded.

Lauren looked at Samantha. The older girl was scuffing one of her trainers across

the ground. Her brown hair hid her face
and it was impossible to guess what she
was thinking. She didn't look at Jessica
once.

'Well,' Mr Parker said, after a pause, 'I
guess we should be getting home.'

'Dad,' Jessica said suddenly, 'can Lauren
come round at the weekend?'

Lauren looked at her in surprise.

'I don't know, Jess,' Mr Parker began,
looking a bit awkward. 'Another time
might be better. We have got Samantha
staying . . .'

Samantha kicked a stone. 'I don't care
if she has a friend to visit.'

'Samantha!' Sally said, and for a
moment Lauren thought she was going

to tell Samantha off. But then Sally's face softened. 'Please don't use that tone of voice,' she said mildly.

Samantha shrugged and kicked the ground again.

'Please, Dad,' Jessica begged.

Her dad looked at Samantha, then sighed. 'OK.' He turned to Lauren. 'You're very welcome to come round tomorrow morning, Lauren – if it's all right with your mum and dad. Now, we'd better go. Come on, Jessica – the car's round the corner.'

As Lauren watched Jessica and her family walk out of sight, she felt a little sad. She wouldn't want to be Jessica this weekend.

★

As soon as Lauren got home from school, she got changed and went outside to catch Twilight. As she groomed him, she told him about Jessica. He couldn't speak to her when he wasn't a unicorn, but she knew he could understand.

'Jessica's so unhappy,' Lauren told him, as she swept the brush over his neck.

Twilight whickered sympathetically.

'I'm going round there tomorrow morning. I just wish there was something I could do to cheer her up,' Lauren said.

Twilight pushed her with his nose. Lauren frowned. She had a feeling he was trying to tell her something. Twilight nudged at his saddle hanging on the fence. Lauren's eyes widened. Of course!

'I can bring Jessica back here tomorrow and she can ride you!' she exclaimed. 'She loves horses. It's bound to cheer her up.'

Twilight nodded as if that was exactly what he'd been trying to say.

CHAPTER
Three

'Hi, Lauren,' Mr Parker said when Lauren arrived at Jessica's house the next morning. 'Jessica's in the kitchen with Sally and Samantha.'

Lauren went through into the large kitchen. Jessica was sitting at the table, drawing a picture of a horse. Samantha was listening to a Walkman. Her eyes were closed.

'Lauren!' Jessica said, jumping up.

Sally was unloading the dishwasher.
'Hi, Lauren. How are you?'

'Fine thanks,' Lauren replied. She
looked at Jessica's drawing. 'I like your
horse.'

'Thanks,' Jessica said, smiling.

'My little artist,' Mr Parker said fondly
as he came to look at her picture.

Jessica shot an embarrassed look at
Lauren. 'Come on, let's go to my
room.'

'Do you want to take some milk and
cookies with you?' Sally asked.

Lauren and Jessica both nodded eagerly
and while Sally poured two glasses of
milk for them, Jessica fetched the cookie

tin. 'Do you want one, Samantha?' she
offered.

But Samantha continued to listen to
her Walkman, her eyes closed.

Sally removed the headphones
from Samantha's ears.

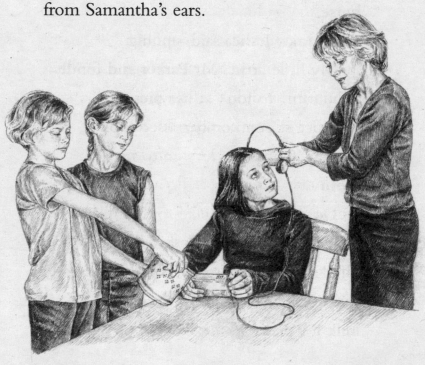

'Mum!' Samantha protested.

'Jessica just asked you if you would like a cookie,' Sally said.

Samantha looked in the tin that Jessica was holding out. 'I don't like any of them,' she said rudely.

Lauren stared. If she'd spoken like that, her mum would have been furious with her, but Sally didn't say anything.

'What sort of cookies do you like then, Samantha?' Mr Parker asked.

Samantha shrugged. 'Pecan and chocolate chip.'

'Well, in that case we should get some when we're out this afternoon,' he said.

'Come on,' Jessica muttered to Lauren. 'Let's go to my room.'

When they reached Jessica's bedroom, Jessica flung herself down on her bed. 'I can't believe how Dad and Sally treat Samantha. She gets her own way about everything. Like this afternoon, Dad's suggested we all go for a game of miniature golf or ten-pin bowling, but no, Samantha doesn't want to do that so we have to spend the afternoon going around the mall instead.' Jessica pulled her knees up to her chest. 'We always do what she wants to do. What's it going to be like after the wedding when she lives here all the time?'

Lauren wanted to comfort her, but she couldn't think of anything to say.

Jessica sniffed and angrily brushed a

tear away from her eyes. 'I'm sorry,' she said.

'It's OK,' Lauren replied. She remembered her plan from the day before. 'Look, why don't we go round to my house and ride Twilight?'

Jessica's eyes lit up. 'Yeah – OK!'

They quickly drank their milk, ate their cookies and took their empty glasses downstairs.

Sally and Samantha were still in the kitchen. Sally was holding Samantha's hands. She broke off as Lauren and Jessica walked in. 'Oh . . . hi, girls.'

Samantha didn't say anything.

Jessica ignored her. 'May Lauren and I go and see Twilight?' she asked Sally.

Sally smiled. 'Sure,' she said. Then she glanced at Samantha. 'Samantha, why don't you go with them? You'd like to see Lauren's pony, wouldn't you?'

Lauren stared at Sally in surprise. This hadn't been part of the plan at all. Anyway, surely Samantha would refuse?

Samantha shrugged. 'I guess I *could* go,' she said.

'I'm sure you'll all have a great time together,' Sally said, beaming happily.

Samantha stood up and looked at Lauren and Jessica. 'Come on, then,' she said abruptly. And with that, she walked out of the kitchen.

Shooting looks of dismay at each other, Lauren and Jessica followed

Samantha outside.

'Where's your house, then?' Samantha said to Lauren.

'About ten minutes away,' Lauren replied. 'It's called Granger's Farm.'

'Right.' Samantha put her headphones on and walked off down the road ahead of them.

'I don't want her to come!' Jessica said to Lauren.

Lauren shook her head, looking at Samantha striding on ahead, and whispered, 'But what can we do?'

CHAPTER

Four

Samantha was waiting for them outside the entrance to Granger's Farm.

'Twilight's down there,' Lauren said, pointing to the path that led round the side of the farmhouse to the paddock.

Samantha shrugged as if she wasn't interested, but followed Lauren and Jessica down the path.

Twilight was standing by the paddock gate. He whinnied as he saw them.

'Oh, he's lovely!' The words burst out of Samantha.

Both Lauren and Jessica turned to stare. Samantha's face had lit up.

'Do you like horses, then?' Jessica asked her.

But the delight was already leaving Samantha's face. She shrugged. 'They're OK,' she said coldly. Then she walked over to the fence and began to kick at a stone.

Lauren decided to ignore her. She fetched Twilight's halter and grooming kit. She and Jessica groomed Twilight together while Samantha leaned against the fence.

However, when Lauren and Jessica
went up to the tack room to fetch
Twilight's saddle and bridle, Lauren saw
Samantha go over to Twilight and stroke
his neck.

Twilight behaved perfectly for Jessica.
He cantered round the paddock and then

jumped over a small fence that Lauren's dad had made.

'Wow!' Jessica said, as she trotted him back to the gate. 'Twilight's great, Lauren. He felt like he was flying when he jumped!'

Twilight gave Lauren a cheeky look from underneath his long forelock.

Jessica dismounted. 'Are you going to have a go now, Lauren?'

Lauren nodded, but as she reached to take Twilight's reins, he stepped forward and snorted in Samantha's direction.

Lauren guessed what he was trying to say. 'Samantha, would you like a ride?' she said.

'Me?' Samantha looked very surprised.

For a moment, Lauren thought she was going to say yes, but then she seemed to think better of it. 'No, no, I won't,' she said abruptly and, crossing her arms, she turned away.

Lauren frowned. She had a feeling Samantha liked horses. But why was she being so unfriendly? She shrugged and glanced at Twilight. He seemed to have a puzzled look on his face too.

Samantha hardly said another word for the rest of the morning. She ignored Lauren and Jessica as they untacked Twilight and brushed him over. 'We should go, Jessica,' she said at last. 'It's almost lunchtime.'

Jessica nodded reluctantly.

As Samantha strode back up the path, Jessica turned to Lauren. 'I wish you were coming with us,' she said. 'The rest of the weekend's going to be awful.'

'It might not be that bad,' Lauren said, trying to cheer her friend up. 'Maybe Samantha will stop being so moody.'

Jessica didn't look convinced.

'Come on, Jessica,' Samantha called irritably from halfway up the drive.

'Bye, Lauren,' Jessica whispered, suddenly sounding as if she was fighting back tears. She gave Twilight a last pat. 'I'd better go.'

Lauren watched her run up the path after Samantha. 'Oh, Twilight,' she said quietly, stroking him. 'I wish we could help.'

That evening, Lauren turned Twilight into a unicorn. 'If only there was something we could do to make Samantha and Jessica get on better,' she said. 'Samantha's so horrid.'

'You know, Samantha was stroking me when you and Jessica weren't there,' Twilight said. 'She was different then. I got the feeling that she was a little sad.'

'But why should she be sad?' Lauren said. 'I mean, I know her mum's getting married again, but Jessica and her dad are really nice.' She frowned. 'And even if she is sad, she shouldn't be so mean to Jessica.

'I know,' Twilight said. 'But it must be hard for Samantha having to move house and adjust to life with a new father and stepsister.'

'I guess,' Lauren reluctantly agreed.

'I think that Samantha's just putting on an act,' Twilight continued. 'I don't think she's really mean. People do strange things when they're unhappy.'

'Well, I wish Samantha would stop it,' Lauren said. 'Jessica's so miserable.'

Twilight nuzzled her. 'Look, why don't we go flying?'

Lauren sighed. 'OK,' she agreed. Maybe that would take her mind off Jessica's problems for a while. 'Let's go to the clearing.'

'OK,' Twilight agreed eagerly.

Lauren climbed on to his back and he cantered upwards into the night sky.

A few minutes later, Twilight flew down between the trees that covered the mountain behind Granger's Farm. He landed lightly on springy grass.

'Wow!' Lauren gasped.

She had never been to the clearing at night before. She had expected it to be dark but it was lit by hundreds of fireflies. They circled and swooped, like tiny moving stars. Lauren slid off Twilight's warm back and breathed in the night air. It was sweet with the heavy scent of the purple flowers that dotted the grass. They were star-shaped and at the tip of each petal a golden spot glowed.

Moonflowers, Lauren thought to herself. She had needed a moonflower when she had first said the spell to turn Twilight into a unicorn. Leaving Twilight, she crouched down and looked at them.

With a soft snort, Twilight moved to the grassy mound at the centre of the clearing. Lowering his head, he began to graze, his long horn touching the grass.

Lauren walked over to him and, for the first time, she noticed that there were some rocks around the base of the mound. In the light from the fireflies they seemed to twinkle and shine with a pink glow. 'Are these magic rocks?' she asked Twilight.

'I don't think so,' Twilight replied. 'They're just made of rose quartz. You find them all through this forest.'

'Oh.' Lauren couldn't help feeling slightly disappointed. She sat down on the grassy mound and watched the fireflies dancing. 'I wonder what Jessica's doing now,' she said. 'I wish I knew.'

'Me too,' said Twilight. As he spoke, his

horn touched one of the pink rocks.
There was a bright purple flash. Twilight
shot backwards with a startled whinny as
mist suddenly started to swirl over the
rock.

Lauren leapt to her feet. 'Twilight!' she
gasped.

Five

Lauren and Twilight stared at the mist in astonishment.

'What's happening?' Lauren asked, clutching Twilight's mane.

'I don't know,' Twilight quickly replied. The mist started fading into the air.

'Look!' Lauren exclaimed. The surface of the rock was shining like a mirror. It had a picture in it. Lauren edged closer.

'There are four people,' she gasped. 'A man, a woman and . . .' She broke off and stared. 'Twilight! It's Jessica's house!'

Twilight moved quickly beside her and together they gazed in astonishment at the image on the rock's surface. It was a picture of the main room at Jessica's house. Mr Parker and Sally were sitting on the sofa talking to Samantha. Jessica was sitting by herself on the floor.

Lauren could hear a low buzzing noise. It sounded like voices coming from far, far away. She leaned nearer to the rock. It was voices! Now she was closer to the picture she could hear what everyone was saying . . .

Sally was speaking to Samantha: 'What

would you like to do tomorrow, darling?'

Lauren saw Samantha shrug. 'Go to the mall,' she replied.

'Oh, not again!' Jessica said.

Lauren saw Sally and Mr Parker exchange anxious looks. 'Maybe we could do something else, Sam,' said Mr Parker.

Samantha's face set in a mutinous line. 'There's nothing else worth doing in this stupid town!' she exclaimed.

Lauren looked round at Twilight. 'This is amazing!' she whispered. 'We're watching what's going on in Jessica's house right now. This rock must be magic after all.'

'Maybe it's not the rock,' Twilight said thoughtfully. 'You said you wished you knew what was going on at Jessica's house and I touched the rock with my horn . . .'

'So maybe it's your horn that's working the magic,' Lauren guessed.

Twilight nodded thoughtfully. 'When I was a foal, my mother used to tell me about the wise Golden Unicorns who rule Arcadia,' he said.

'That's the land where all the magic creatures live, isn't it?' Lauren asked, remembering that she had read about Arcadia in the unicorn book she owned.

'Yes,' Twilight replied. 'My mother told me that there are seven Golden Unicorns. They watch over the mortal world using a stone table that shines like a mirror when they touch it with their horns.'

'So, you mean this could be one of

your magical powers?' Lauren asked.

Twilight nodded again. 'Maybe I can see what's going on in other places if I touch a rock with my horn and say what I wish to see.'

'Any rock?' Lauren said excitedly.

'I don't know,' Twilight replied. 'But I guess there's one way to find out.' He trotted to the edge of the clearing where there was a boulder of plain grey granite. 'What shall we try to see?'

'My house,' Lauren suggested.

'I wish I could see Lauren's house,' Twilight said, touching his horn to the stone.

Nothing happened.

'Maybe it's just when you touch a rock

made out of rose quartz, then,' Lauren said.

Twilight cantered to one of the other pinky-grey rocks and touched his horn to it. 'I wish I could see Lauren's house,' he said.

There was a purple flash and mist started swirling over the rock.

'It's worked!' Lauren gasped. She ran over. As the mist cleared, she saw that the rock's surface was shining. An image of the outside of her house was slowly forming, blurry at first but getting sharper by the second. 'Wow!' she whispered. She could see her dad's car, the path to Twilight's paddock and Buddy, Max's Bernese mountain dog

puppy, sniffing round outside Twilight's
stable.

Twilight touched his horn to the rock
again and, with a slight popping noise,
the picture disappeared.

Lauren went back to the first rock. The picture of Jessica's house was as clear as if she were watching it on television. Jessica was standing up now, looking very upset.

'I don't want to go shopping again tomorrow!' she said.

Her dad sighed. 'Well, we're going to. It's what Samantha wants to do.'

Jessica glared at him. 'Why do we always have to do what she wants, Dad?' she exclaimed, shooting an angry look at Samantha who was sitting on the sofa ignoring her. 'It's not fair!'

'That's enough, Jessica!' Mr Parker spoke firmly.

Lauren saw Jessica bite back a reply and run from the room.

Mr Parker ran a hand through his hair.
'I'd better go and talk to her,' he said.

Lauren turned to Twilight. 'Oh, I wish
we could help her. Can't you do
anything?'

'But what?' Twilight answered.

'I don't know,' Lauren admitted. She
thought hard. 'Maybe Mrs Fontana will
help us think of something.'

Mrs Fontana owned a bookshop and
knew all about Twilight's unicorn magic.

Twilight nodded eagerly. 'Good idea!'

Lauren glanced at the rock again. Sally
had her arm round Samantha and was
talking to her. Lauren started to lean
forward to listen to what Sally was saying
and then changed her mind. It somehow

seemed wrong to listen in on a private
conversation.

'Please make it go away, Twilight,' she
said.

He touched the picture with his horn
and it disappeared. Despite the light from
the dancing fireflies, the clearing suddenly
seemed much darker.

'Come on,' Lauren said, taking hold of
Twilight's mane and scrambling on to his
back. 'We ought to go home.'

CHAPTER
Six

The next morning, Lauren pushed open the old-fashioned door that led into Mrs Fontana's bookshop. A chime jangled and Walter, Mrs Fontana's black and white terrier, trotted over to meet her, his tail wagging. As Lauren patted him, Mrs Fontana appeared from the back of the shop.

'Hello, Lauren, this is a nice surprise,'

she said, coming over, a smile crinkling
up her lined face. As always, her long
grey hair was pinned up in a bun and
she had a mustard-yellow shawl around
her shoulders. 'So, what can I do for
you?'

Lauren glanced round, wondering
whether it was safe to talk.

'It's OK,' Mrs Fontana said. 'You're the
only person here.' Her bright blue eyes
searched Lauren's face. 'I take it this visit
is about Twilight?'

Lauren nodded.

'Why don't we sit down?' Mrs Fontana
said, waving to one of the armchairs that
nestled among the piles of books – new
and second-hand – that rose from the

floor like wobbly towers. 'So, tell me,'
Mrs Fontana said, sitting opposite her.
'What's the problem?'

Lauren explained about Jessica and then about the night before in the clearing. As she explained how Twilight's horn made the picture appear in the rose quartz rock, Mrs Fontana chuckled.

'That must have given you a shock,' she said.

'Yes, it did,' Lauren said, grinning.

'That was always one of my favourite unicorn powers.' A smile played across the old lady's face and Lauren had the sudden feeling that Mrs Fontana was reliving old memories. With a blink, Mrs Fontana seemed to come back to the present. 'So, what is it you want to know?'

'Can Twilight help my friend?' Lauren said.

'Of course he can!' Mrs Fontana smiled. 'But I can't tell you how. You and Twilight must learn how to use his powers for yourself. With your good heart and his courage, I know you'll find a way.'

Lauren felt disappointed. 'But I've been thinking and thinking what we can do,' she said, 'and I still don't know. Is there anything you can suggest?'

Mrs Fontana's voice dropped and she leaned forward. 'It might help you to know that there is a way that someone else can see Twilight. If a person drinks the Unseeing Potion, it will make them forget they have ever seen a unicorn. However,' her eyes seemed to bore into

Lauren, 'the Unseeing Potion will only work if it is taken knowingly and willingly. You can only reveal Twilight's secret to someone you can trust to drink the potion. If you reveal his secret to the wrong person, then his life could be put in danger.'

Lauren's thoughts were spinning – a potion that meant someone else could see Twilight safely. That was amazing! A thought struck her. 'But I don't see how this helps Jessica,' she said.

Mrs Fontana smiled. 'As I said, how you use Twilight's powers is up to you.' She seemed to see the frustration on Lauren's face. 'Oh, my dear, please believe me, I am not trying to make your life

difficult.' She took Lauren's hands. 'There
is a reason why I cannot tell you what
Twilight's powers are or how he should
use them.'

'But what is it?' Lauren said.

Mrs Fontana's blue gaze met hers. 'One
day, you will find out.'

Just then Walter gave a sharp bark. Mrs
Fontana glanced at the door. 'There is
someone coming,' she said quickly. 'We
cannot talk any more now. Use the
advice I have given you wisely, my dear.
Promise me you will take great care
before you reveal Twilight's secret to
anyone.'

'I will,' Lauren promised.

The shop door opened and Mrs Foster

looked in, holding armfuls of shopping
bags. 'Hello, Mrs Fontana,' she said,
smiling. 'Ah, there you are, Lauren,' she
said, catching sight of Lauren sitting in
the chair. 'I've bought the things I needed
from town. Are you ready to go?'

Lauren nodded and got to her feet.
'Bye, Mrs Fontana.'

'Goodbye, Lauren,' Mrs Fontana
replied. Her eyes twinkled. 'No doubt I'll
see you again soon.'

As Lauren reached the door, Mrs
Fontana came after her. 'Oh, Lauren. You
might need this.' She pressed a folded
piece of paper into Lauren's hand.

'Thanks,' Lauren said, wondering what
the note was.

Lauren read the first few words as they walked to the car: *Take two moonflowers and a hair from a unicorn's mane* . . .

It was the Unseeing Potion!

'What's that, honey?' her mum asked.

Lauren quickly folded the paper up and put it in her pocket. 'Oh nothing,' she said quickly. 'Nothing important.'

CHAPTER
Seven

'I'm going to take Twilight out for a ride,' Lauren said to her mum when they got back home.

It only took her ten minutes to give Twilight a quick brush over and tack him up. 'Just wait till you hear what I've got to tell you,' she said, as she pulled down the stirrups and mounted. 'Come on – we're going to the clearing.'

Sensing her excitement, Twilight pulled
at the bit. As soon as they had trotted out
of the farm and on to the track that led
into the wood, Lauren leaned forward
and let Twilight canter. His hooves
thudded along the sandy track until they
reached the hidden path that led to the
clearing.

At the end of the path, the trees parted
and Twilight trotted into the open space.
Shafts of sunlight shone down through
the leafy canopy and lit up the grass. Pink
and yellow butterflies fluttered through
the air. Lauren stopped Twilight and slid
off. 'I'm going to turn you into a
unicorn,' she told him, as she started to
untack him. 'I know it's daytime but no

one can see us here and we need to talk.'

Twilight nodded his head and snorted as if he agreed.

'OK,' said Lauren, sliding the saddle off his back and putting it on the grass. 'Here goes.'

A few moments later, Twilight was a unicorn. It felt strange for Lauren. Until now, she'd only ever said the spell in the evening. It didn't seem right to have the sun shining down on his snowy-white coat and silvery horn. But Twilight didn't seem to find anything odd about it at all.

'So what did Mrs Fontana say?' he asked.

'She gave me this,' Lauren replied,

getting the piece of paper out of her
pocket. She read out what Mrs Fontana
had written:

Take two moonflowers and a
hair from a unicorn's mane
and put them in water under
the light of the moon. After
ten seconds, the flowers and
the hair will have dissolved in
the water and the potion will
be ready to drink. Within
thirty seconds, the person who
has drunk it will have
forgotten they have ever seen
a unicorn.

'So if someone drinks the potion they won't remember having seen me?' Twilight said.

'That's right,' Lauren told him.

'But what would happen if the person changed their mind and decided not to drink the potion?' Twilight said.

'Mrs Fontana said that was a risk,' Lauren replied. 'She told me that we have to be very careful about whom we choose to reveal your secret to.'

'But I don't understand how it would help Jessica to be able to see me,' said Twilight.

Lauren sighed. 'Neither do I. But I'm sure Mrs Fontana wouldn't have given us the recipe unless it could help. I guess

we've just got to think about it a bit
longer.' She glanced round. Although the
glade was the most secret place she could

think of, there was still a chance that
someone might come along. 'We'd better
turn back now. I'll come and visit you
tonight and we'll see if we can think of a
plan then.'

'OK,' Twilight agreed.

Lauren kissed his nose and then said
the words of the Undoing Spell. There
was a purple flash and Twilight was a
pony once more.

As Lauren rode back along the main
forest track, she glanced at her watch. She
might as well ride Twilight for a little bit
longer.

'Let's go to Jessica's,' she said to
Twilight. 'We won't stop for long but it

might cheer her up to see us.'

Twilight nodded and they trotted along the road to Jessica's house.

Sally was watering the pots of flowers at the front of the house. 'Hello, Lauren,' she said, smiling as Lauren turned Twilight into the driveway. 'Have you come to see Jessica?'

'Yes,' Lauren said, thinking how nice she was. 'I just thought I'd say hi.'

'I'll go and get her,' Sally said. 'And maybe your pony would like some water? I could fetch a bucket from the back yard.'

'That would be great,' Lauren said, smiling at her and dismounting.

Sally went into the house. A minute

later, Jessica came running out of the
front door. 'Lauren! Sally said you were
here! Oh, Twilight,' she said, giving him a
hug. He nuzzled her, leaving a messy
mark on her T-shirt. Jessica grinned, not
seeming to mind a bit.

'It's really good to see you,' she said to
Lauren.

'How's it going?' Lauren asked her
anxiously. Although Jessica was smiling
now, her eyes looked suspiciously red, as
if she'd recently been crying.

'Oh, it's not too bad,' Jessica said. She
spoke bravely, but Lauren could tell she
was upset. 'I've got to go and try a
bridesmaid's dress on this afternoon,'
Jessica continued. She swallowed, then

burst out, 'Oh, Lauren, I just don't want the wedding to happen! Samantha was so mean last night.'

Lauren only just stopped herself from saying 'I know'.

'Er . . . how?' she asked.

'Oh, the usual,' Jessica said. 'I got a bit mad and Dad came to talk to me. He said I've got to try and be more understanding. He said that he knows Samantha seems difficult to get on with but it's just because she's upset about leaving her school and friends to come and live here. But I think it's because she just doesn't like me!'

'Of course she does,' Lauren started to say. 'Maybe your dad has a point —'

'But she *doesn't* like me, Lauren!' Jessica interrupted, her blue eyes welling with tears. 'And I don't want to have to live with her!'

Just then the back gate opened and Sally came out with a bucket of water and a couple of carrots. 'Here we are,' she said cheerfully. 'I thought he might be hungry as well.'

'Thanks,' Lauren said, glancing at Jessica, who had hidden her face from Sally by stroking Twilight's neck.

'Well,' Sally said, putting down the bucket. 'I'll leave you two to it, then. Don't stay out here too long, Jessica. Remember we've got the bridesmaid's dress fitting this afternoon.'

Jessica nodded.

As Sally went inside, Lauren looked anxiously at Jessica. 'Are you OK?'

Jessica sniffed. 'I guess I'll have to be,' she said in a small voice. 'See you, Lauren.

How I wish this wedding wasn't happening!'

Lauren sighed. If only she could think of some way of helping . . .

The minutes seemed to crawl by so slowly until the evening. Lauren was longing to be able to go and talk things over with Twilight. As soon as she and Max had finished filling the dishwasher with their dirty plates, Lauren put her trainers on. 'I'm just going to see Twilight,' she said to her parents.

'OK, honey,' her dad said. He looked under the kitchen table, where Max was playing with Buddy. 'Come on, Max. Time for your bath.'

Just as he and Max were going up the stairs, the phone rang. 'Lauren, can you get that for me, please?' he called.

Lauren jumped to her feet and picked up the receiver. 'Granger's Farm. Who's speaking, please?'

'Lauren. It's Jessica's dad here.' Mr Parker's voice was tense and tight, and in the background Lauren was sure she could hear someone crying.

'Oh, hello,' Lauren started to say, wondering why he was ringing. 'Do you want to speak to my −'

Mr Parker cut her off. 'Lauren, have you seen Jessica in the last couple of hours?'

Lauren frowned. 'No. Why?'

'She's gone missing,' Mr Parker said.
'We think she's run away!'

CHAPTER

Eight

For a moment, Lauren was too shocked to speak. 'Run away!' she stammered at last.

'Can I speak to your father, please?' Mr Parker asked.

'Dad!' Lauren shouted.

Mr Foster came hurrying down the stairs. 'What's the matter?' he asked, seeing her pale face.

'Jessica's run away!' Lauren exclaimed.

Her dad took the phone. Lauren's legs felt shaky and she sat down at the table. It was still light outside at the moment, but soon it would get dark. What would Jessica do then?

'I'll come over and help you look, Jack,' she heard her father saying quickly. 'I'll tell Alice what's happening. She can ring if Jessica turns up here.' There was a pause and then Mr Foster nodded. 'Sure. I'll be with you as soon as I can.'

He put the phone down.

'Can I come with you?' Lauren asked, jumping to her feet.

'I think it's best if you stay here,' Mr Foster said. 'Everyone at the Parkers' is

very upset just now – particularly
Samantha. Mr Parker said she seems to
think it's all her fault.'

Mr Foster saw the worry on his
daughter's face and gave her a quick hug.
'It'll be all right,' he said comfortingly.
'We'll find Jessica. Don't you worry.'

Five minutes later, Lauren was alone in
the kitchen. Her mum and Max were
upstairs and her dad had gone to the
Parkers'. She went to the window and
stared out into the dusk. If only she knew
where Jessica was.

And it was then that an idea struck
her. Of course! Twilight's magic powers
could show her. They only had to look

into the rock. Why hadn't she thought of
it before?

She pulled open the door and raced
outside.

'Twilight!' she cried, running down the
path to the paddock. 'Quick! I need your
help.'

Twilight was already standing by the
gate. He began to whinny frantically.

'Jessica's gone missing,' she gasped. 'We
need to go to the wood and –'

A neigh from Twilight cut across her
words. He reared up, his front hooves
stamping down on the grass.

'What's the matter?' Lauren asked in
astonishment. The only other time she'd
ever seen him looking so agitated was

when Max and Buddy had almost caught her turning him into a unicorn. Her eyes suddenly widened. Maybe there was someone nearby?

She spun around, half-expecting to see someone, but there were only the familiar shapes of the trees and bushes, shadowy against the night sky.

'What is it?' she asked Twilight.

Twilight stamped his front hoof. Lauren listened. In the silence, she heard a sudden rustle.

Her heart almost jumped out of her chest. The noise had come from a large bush near the gate. Taking a deep breath, she walked forward. 'Hello,' she called, trying to sound brave. 'Is there anyone there?'

Through the silence of the night came the sound of a sob. Lauren ran forward, suddenly no longer afraid. She reached into the bush and pushed the branches aside.

'Jessica!' she gasped.

Jessica was crouching in the hollow centre of the bush. Her face was streaked with tears. When she saw Lauren she buried her head in her hands and sobbed again.

'What are you doing here?' Lauren asked.

Jessica showed no signs of answering and so Lauren pushed her way through the brambles towards her. 'Please come

out.' She put an arm around Jessica's
shoulders and helped her out of the bush.
Twilight came over and nuzzled Jessica's
cold hands.

'Everyone's looking for you,' Lauren
said, staring at her friend. 'What's wrong?'

'Everything.' Jessica put her arms round
Twilight's neck and buried her face in his
mane. 'I don't want to go home ever
again, Lauren.'

'Why? What's happened?' Lauren
asked.

Jessica sniffed. 'This afternoon was
awful. We went to try the bridesmaids'
dresses on and Samantha refused to have
the shoes or headdresses that we had
chosen and made out that I'm just a little

kid who doesn't know anything. Then she wouldn't speak to her mum because Sally said that my opinion did matter. Worst of all, when we got home, Dad said he and Sally have decided that when Samantha moves in after the wedding, she's going to share my bedroom.'

'Share your bedroom!' Lauren echoed.

Jessica nodded. 'Dad says that they think it will help us get to know each other better. But I don't want to get to know Samantha,' she wailed. 'She hates me and I bet she's glad I've run away.'

Lauren shook her head. 'She's not – she's really upset.'

'As if,' Jessica said.

'She is,' Lauren insisted. 'Your dad said.'

'It's just an act, then,' Jessica said. 'She doesn't care about me at all.' And with that, she began to cry again.

Lauren hugged her, wishing that she could show Jessica that Samantha did care.

Twilight whinnied. Lauren looked at him. He turned to look in the direction of the wood.

Lauren caught her breath. Of course! There actually was a way that she could show Jessica that Samantha was upset. But it would mean revealing Twilight's secret.

Leaving Jessica for a moment, Lauren went over to Twilight. 'Are you sure?' she whispered into his ear.

Twilight whickered softly and nodded his head.

'OK,' Lauren told him. She turned to her friend. 'Jessica, I'm sure I can prove that Samantha really does care about you.'

Jessica frowned. 'How?'

'I'll tell you in a second,' Lauren said. 'But first you have to promise that afterwards you'll do whatever I ask.'

'All right,' Jessica said. 'I promise.'

Lauren swallowed. 'OK.' She took Jessica's hand. 'Look, don't be shocked, but Twilight isn't just a pony, Jessica. He's . . . well . . .' she took a deep breath, 'he's a unicorn.'

For a moment, Jessica looked at her in stunned silence and then, despite her unhappiness, she laughed. 'A unicorn!' she said. 'Don't be silly, Lauren!'

'No, he is,' Lauren said.

Jessica stared at her. 'Unicorns don't exist. They're just make-believe —'

'Just watch,' Lauren interrupted. She swung round and quickly said the magic spell and suddenly Twilight was standing there — a unicorn once more.

Lauren thought Jessica was going to faint.

'But . . . but . . .' Jessica stammered, staring at him, her eyes wide.

'See, unicorns do exist,' Lauren said.

Jessica walked slowly to Twilight. 'He's so beautiful!' With a shaking hand she reached out and touched his neck. 'Oh, wow!' she breathed. 'Just wait till everyone hears about this!'

'You can't tell anyone, Jessica,' Lauren said quickly. 'It has to be a secret.'

Jessica frowned. 'But I don't understand,' she said.

'We'll talk about it later,' Lauren said. Time was passing and with every minute that went by she knew that Jessica's family would be feeling more and more worried. First she had to carry out her plan, then she and Twilight had to get Jessica home as quickly as they could. She looked at Twilight. 'Can you carry us both?'

'Yes, of course,' Twilight said.

Jessica almost jumped out of her skin. 'He can talk!' she exclaimed.

'Yes, but you can only hear him if you're touching him or holding a hair from his mane,' Lauren told her. She saw Jessica's mouth start to open with a question. 'Come on, I'll explain on the way.'

As Twilight flew to the clearing in the wood, Lauren told Jessica all about unicorns and how she had discovered Twilight's secret. Jessica was thrilled. 'So there are other unicorns in the world?' she said as Twilight began to fly down through the trees.

'Yes,' Lauren said. 'But they just look like grey ponies. They can only turn into a unicorn if they find someone who believes in magic enough to say the Turning Spell.'

'Like you did,' Jessica said as Twilight

landed on the soft grass.

Lauren nodded and dismounted.

'I'd give anything to have a unicorn of my own,' Jessica said longingly. She slid off Twilight's back and looked around at the fireflies dancing through the dusky air. 'What a cool place,' she breathed. 'But why are we here?'

'We're going to show you how Samantha feels about you being missing,' Lauren said, walking over to one of the pinky-grey rocks. She desperately hoped that her plan was going to work.

Twilight joined her. 'I wish I could see Samantha,' she said, and Twilight touched the stone with his horn.

Jessica gasped as the purple light

flashed and mist started to swirl. She
grabbed Lauren's arm.

'It's OK,' Lauren told her. 'Watch what
happens now.'

Just as before, the mist slowly cleared
to show the surface of the rock
beginning to shine like a mirror. As they
watched, two shadowy shapes in the
mirror gradually became clearer.

'It's Samantha and Sally!' Jessica
exclaimed in astonishment.

The mirror showed a picture of the
kitchen at Jessica's house. Samantha and
her mum were sitting at the table.

'You need to get close to be able to
hear what they're saying,' Lauren said
to Jessica.

They crouched down together.

'She's been out for hours now, Mum,' Samantha was sobbing. 'What if she doesn't come back?'

'She will,' Sally soothed, stroking her hair. 'I'm sure Jack will find her soon.'

'But what if he doesn't? Oh, Mum, it's all my fault,' Samantha cried. 'I was so mean to her. I wish I hadn't been. It's just I've been so scared about coming to live here. It's Jessica's life and Jessica's house and I feel like an outsider.'

'I know, Sam,' her mum said. 'But our house is too far away from Jack's work for us to live there.' She stroked her hair. 'I promise it won't take you long to settle in and make new friends here. And I'm sure Jessica will help you.'

'If she ever comes back,' Samantha said. 'What if something bad has happened to her?' More tears spilled out of her eyes.

'Oh, Mum, I'm so worried about her.'

Sally hugged her tight, but as she lifted her eyes upwards Lauren could see how strained and worried she looked.

Lauren glanced at Jessica. Her face was pale and shocked. Lauren reached out and took her hand. 'See? It won't be that bad when your dad and Sally get married,' she said softly. 'And maybe having a sister will be fun.'

Jessica swallowed hard and looked at Twilight. 'Can you show me what it will be like?' she asked.

Twilight shook his head. 'No one can see into the future, not even unicorns.' He nuzzled her shoulder. 'The future's up to you, Jessica. It's what you make it. But

now you know how Samantha feels, I'm
sure it can all work out — if you want it to.'

Jessica took a deep breath. 'I want it to,'
she said. She glanced at the mirror again.
'There's Dad,' she said suddenly. 'Look!'

Mr Parker had just come into the
picture. Lauren and Jessica both bent
forward to hear what was going on.

Sally had jumped to her feet. 'Have
you found her?'

Mr Parker shook his head. 'I thought
I'd check back here to see if she's called.'

Sally shook her head. 'No . . . no, she
hasn't.'

Mr Parker ran his hand through his
hair. 'Where is she?' he groaned. 'It's this
wedding. I know it is.'

'Perhaps we should call it off,' Sally said, looking worried.

'No!' Jessica exclaimed. She looked at Lauren and Twilight. Her eyes were suddenly glinting with tears. 'Take me home, Twilight,' she said. 'Please!'

CHAPTER
Nine

As Jessica clambered on to Twilight's snowy-white back, Lauren bent down and picked two purple moonflowers from the grass. She felt a flutter of fear. Was Jessica going to keep her promise to do whatever Lauren asked when they dropped her back home?

The flight home was tense. Lauren could sense how anxious Jessica was to let her family know that she was safe. It seemed like forever before Twilight landed gently under the cover of some trees near Jessica's house.

'We need to wait a moment,' Lauren told Jessica as they dismounted.

'But I want to get home as quickly as possible,' Jessica said.

'It'll only take a minute,' Lauren assured her. 'We need to do something.'

'What?' Jessica asked.

Lauren took a deep breath. 'Well, you remember that before I turned Twilight into a unicorn I made you promise that you would do whatever I asked?' she said.

'Yes,' Jessica said.

'Well, you've got to drink a potion that

will make you forget you've ever seen Twilight. That's what this water is for,' she said, taking a little bottle out of her pocket. 'It's to make the potion.'

'I won't remember anything about him at all?' Jessica said a little sadly.

Lauren shook her head.

'But . . . but . . .' Jessica seemed lost for words.

'It's to keep him safe,' Lauren said. 'If anyone else knows about him, he could be in real danger.'

'I think I understand,' Jessica said slowly.

'So you'll drink the potion?' Lauren asked her.

Jessica nodded. 'Yes,' she said.

'Well, all I need to do is add the

flowers and a hair of Twilight's mane to this water,' Lauren said. 'And then we put it in the moonlight for ten seconds and it's ready to drink.'

She broke off a single hair from Twilight's mane and dropped it into the bottle with the two flowers. The water immediately fizzed and bubbled and turned purple. Lauren held it up to a shaft of moonlight that was filtering down through the trees. As they watched, the purple faded and the liquid became clear. A sweet smell floated off it, like lemonade.

'It's ready,' Lauren said, after she had counted to ten. She held the bottle out to Jessica.

Jessica stroked the unicorn's neck.
'Goodbye, Twilight,' she said softly.
Twilight blew gently on her face and

then she took the bottle. 'Here goes,' she
said, and in one gulp she drained the
liquid.

Lauren watched her. She sort of
expected something to happen – a purple
flash or something – but nothing did.

'Thank you,' Jessica said, handing the
bottle back to Lauren. 'It tasted sort of
sweet and fruity.' She frowned. 'But it
hasn't made me forget about Twilight.'

'The spell said that it takes thirty
seconds to work,' Twilight said.

Lauren looked towards the house.
'You'd better go,' she said to Jessica. The
curtains hadn't been drawn across the
kitchen windows and she could see Mr
Parker pacing up and down while Sally

hugged Samantha at the kitchen table. 'Everyone's worried about you. Let them know you're all right.'

'OK,' Jessica said. 'Bye!' And with that she began to run across the lawn. But just as she reached the back door, she stopped.

'What's she doing?' Lauren whispered to Twilight as Jessica looked round in a confused way.

'I think the potion's just worked,' he said softly.

As they watched, Jessica shook her head and ran on into the house.

From the shelter of the trees, Twilight and Lauren watched the kitchen window. They saw the worry on Mr Parker's face clear in an instant as Jessica ran into the room. Sally and Samantha jumped to their feet in relief. And they saw Jessica being pulled into a big family hug.

Lauren swallowed the lump of happy tears in her throat. 'Oh, Twilight, I think life's going to be better for Jessica from now on,' she said.

He stamped his hoof. 'I think you're right,' he replied.

Two weeks later, Lauren rode Twilight up to Jessica's house. A big white car was parked in their driveway and, as Lauren halted Twilight to have a look at it, the front door of the house opened and Jessica and Samantha ran out. They were dressed in cream bridesmaids' dresses and they were smiling.

'They're never going to get there on time,' Lauren heard Samantha say.

'Dad's always late!' Jessica said to Samantha.

'That makes two of them,' Samantha told her.

Jessica laughed. Lauren didn't think she'd ever seen her friend look happier. 'Dad! We're going to be late!' Jessica shouted.

The door opened wider and Sally and Mr Parker appeared. Sally was dressed in a beautiful light blue dress and Mr Parker was wearing a smart grey suit.

'Come on!' Jessica insisted, getting hold

of her dad's arm and dragging him to
the car.

Just then Sally caught sight of Lauren.
'Hi!' she called, waving. 'Jessica –
it's Lauren!'

Jessica came racing over.

'Lauren! Lauren!' she gasped. 'Dad's just told me the best news. He's going to get me and Samantha a pony as a wedding present. It turns out she loves horses just as much as I do!'

'That's brilliant!' Lauren exclaimed.

Mr Parker beeped the car's horn. 'Jessica! You'll make us late!'

Jessica looked indignant. 'Me? Make you late!'

Samantha leaned out of the window. 'Hi, Lauren. Come on, Jessica!'

'I'd better go,' Jessica said to Lauren. She reached to pat Twilight goodbye and suddenly a puzzled look crossed her face. She frowned, almost as if she was trying to remember something. 'You know, I had this really funny dream about Twilight . . .' she began.

The car's horn sounded. Jessica's expression cleared. 'Oh, it doesn't matter,' she said, shaking her head. 'See you in school!' And with that she ran to the car.

As Jessica got in, Lauren waved and Twilight whinnied. Then the car pulled out of the driveway and set off down the road.

Lauren looked at Twilight and smiled. Their secret was safe. Once again, only she knew that her pony was a unicorn in disguise.

My Secret Unicorn

There are rumours going round school that there is a haunted treehouse by the creek. It's up to Lauren and Twilight to solve the spooky mystery!

Look out for more *My Secret Unicorn* adventures

My Secret Unicorn

On one of their evening fly-arounds Twilight starts
to feel ill and he and Lauren have to stop exploring
and return home. Can they find something stronger
than magic to help Twilight get bettter. . .?

Look out for more *My Secret Unicorn* adventures

My Secret Unicorn

When Lauren recites a secret spell, her pony
Twilight turns into a beautiful unicorn with magical
powers! Together Lauren and Twilight learn how to
use their magic to help their friends.

Look out for more **My Secret Unicorn** adventures

Cover illustrations © Andrew Farley